HANS DE BEER was born in Muiden, near Amsterdam, Holland. After briefly studying history, he finished his studies at the Rietveld Art Academy in Amsterdam. *Little Polar Bear*, Hans's art school graduation project, brought him worldwide success and countless awards, and has been translated into thirty languages so far. Today Hans lives and works as a freelance illustrator with his wife, the Italian illustrator Serena Romanelli, in Amsterdam and near Florence, Italy.

For my parents

Copyright © 1990 by NordSüd Verlag AG, CH-8050 Zürich, Switzerland.
First published in Switzerland under the title *Kleiner Eisbär – Nimm mich mit, Lars!*
English text copyright © 1990 by NorthSouth Books, Inc., New York 10016.

First published in the United States, Great Britain, Canada, Australia, and New Zealand in 1990 by NorthSouth Books, Inc., an imprint of NordSüd Verlag AG, CH-8005 Zürich, Switzerland. This edition published in 2021.

Distributed in the United States by NorthSouth Books, Inc., New York 10016.
Library of Congress Cataloging-in-Publication Data is available.

ISBN: 978-0-7358-4450-6 (trade edition)
1 3 5 7 9 • 10 8 6 4 2

Printed in Germany by Grafisches Centrum Cuno GmbH & Co. KG, 2020.

www.northsouth.com

Hans de Beer

LITTLE POLAR BEAR

Finds a Friend

North
South

Lars, the little polar bear, was very lonely. As he gazed across the cool blue ocean, he wished he had a friend to play with.

When he got home, Lars's mother could tell right away that something was wrong.

"Why are you so sad?" she asked.

"Because I have no friends here," said Lars glumly.

"Don't worry," said his mother. "One day you'll find someone to play with."

The next morning when Lars went out for a walk, he thought he saw another little polar bear, standing next to a big wooden box.

"I should go over and say hello," thought Lars. But when he got closer he realized that the polar bear was made of wood.

Lars smelled food, so he walked into the box to see what it was. Suddenly there was a loud bang, and the door on the end of the box snapped shut.

Lars was trapped!

It was so dark inside the box that Lars couldn't see a thing. He threw himself against the door, but it wouldn't open.

Lars sat in the box for hours. He thought about his parents and how worried they must have been when he didn't come home.

Suddenly he heard voices outside. The box began to move, and Lars felt it being lifted.

He was very scared. The box bumped up and down and rocked back and forth for another hour. When it finally stopped moving Lars cried out, but no one opened the door.

Then the box began to shake, and Lars heard a loud roar. He felt as if he was being pushed downward and backward, and there was a funny feeling in his tummy. Then the feeling passed. Lars was now very tired, so he curled up in the box and fell asleep.

The next thing Lars knew there was a loud crash, and at last the door to the box burst open. Lars found himself in a strange place filled with many wooden boxes and lots of strange smells.

"Hey, little polar bear, come over here," said a deep, friendly voice.

Lars looked up and was startled to see a huge walrus. "What are you doing here?" asked Lars.

"I was trapped, just like you," said the walrus. "The owl says that we're being taken to a zoo."

"What's a zoo?" asked Lars.

"I don't know," grunted the walrus, "and I don't want to find out. Do you think you could lift the latch on this cage?"

Lars banged the latch with his paws, and finally it swung open. The walrus lumbered out of his cage, and together they started to free all the other animals.

As the cages were opened, Lars was surrounded by many animals he had never seen before. But the biggest surprise came out of the last box: a little brown bear whose name was Bea.

The walrus was very clever, and soon he had found a way to escape. But all the animals were so happy to be free that they ran away, leaving the slow walrus behind.

"Wait for me!" he cried after them.

When Lars and Bea heard the walrus cry, they stopped, turned around, and went back to help their friend. "I'm sorry we ran off," said Lars. "We started together and we'll finish together."

By the time the three of them reached the woods it was dark. They barely escaped being caught in the bright glare of the searchlights. When they were deep in the woods and out of danger, Lars, Bea, and the walrus fell fast asleep.

The next morning when Lars woke up he was surprised to hear Bea crying. "What's wrong?" asked Lars. "We're not in danger anymore."

"It's my parents," sobbed Bea. "They were captured earlier, and I'll probably never see them again."

"I'm sorry," said Lars. But then he had an idea. "Why don't you come home with me!" he said happily. "You can be my sister."

"But won't your parents be upset because I'm brown?" asked Bea.

"Of course not," said Lars. "Bears are bears!"

When the walrus woke up, the three of them talked about how they would get home. "If we could ever find a river," said the walrus, "I could carry the two of you on my back."

While the walrus talked, Bea noticed some bees flying around a tree. "I'm hungry!" Bea said, turning to Lars. "Will you help me get some honey?"

Lars had never seen bees before and he was afraid. He hid behind some bushes with the walrus.

Lars and the walrus liked the honey very much, and as soon as they had eaten, the three friends set off to find a river. As they walked along, Lars couldn't believe how many trees there were in the forest.

Luckily, Bea had such a good sense of smell that she quickly led them to a small stream. The walrus jumped right in and rolled around.

"This feels great," he said happily. "Climb on my back and let's get going!"

As the walrus swam along, the stream turned into a river. Lars told Bea all about his wonderful home.

Then Lars noticed a familiar smell. "We're coming to a city," he said. "I visited a city once. We must be very careful. Let's stop until it gets dark."

While the three of them sat on the riverbank and waited for the sun to go down, Lars told them about his adventure in the city. "I met some nice cats," he said. "But everything is very dirty. My home is much nicer than a city."

The next day, Lars and the walrus recognized the smell of salty seawater. "We're almost home," Lars said to Bea.

"Not quite," said the walrus. "We still have far to go. And first we have to pass through those big gates up ahead."

Soon they found themselves in the middle of the ocean. A storm had started, and the waves were getting bigger and bigger.

"Hang on tight!" yelled the walrus.

At last, the three friends arrived in the Arctic. Bea stared at the strange landscape. She had seen snow before, but she had never seen so much of it.

The walrus dropped Lars and Bea off near Lars's home. It was time to say good-bye.

"Thanks for waiting for me," said the walrus. "I never would have made it home without you."

"And we never would have made it home without you," said Lars.

As the walrus swam away, Lars and Bea set out to find Lars's parents. Bea was having trouble walking on the ice and snow. She kept slipping and sliding.

Suddenly Lars saw his parents and ran up to greet them. Bea slid along behind him.

"Where have you been?" said his mother. "We were so worried about you."

Lars quickly told his parents about his latest adventure and explained that Bea had been separated from her parents.

"She's afraid that you won't let her stay because she's brown," said Lars.

"That's silly," said Lars's father. "Bears are bears."

Lars's mother gave Bea a big hug. "You're a very beautiful bear," she said. "You can stay with us as long as you like."

Lars was very happy. "I can't wait to get home," he said. "There are so many things I want to show my new friend!"